LONG SHOT

A John Rockne Mystery

DAN AMES

LONG SHOT

A John Rockne Mystery

by

Dan Ames

FOREWORD

Do you want more killer crime fiction, along with the chance to win free books? Then sign up for the DAN AMES BOOK CLUB at:

AuthorDanAmes.com

with an engaging narrator and a rich cast of original supporting characters."

-New York Times bestselling author Thomas Perry

"In DEAD WOOD, Dan Ames pulls off a very difficult thing: he re-imagines what a hardboiled mystery can be, and does it with style, thrills and humor. This is the kind of book mystery readers are clamoring for, a fast-paced story with great heart and not a cliché to be found. DEAD WOOD is a hell of a book."

–Amazon.com

Dan Ames' writing reminds me of the great thriller writers -- lean, mean, no nonsense prose that gets straight to the point and keeps you turning those pages."

–author Robert Gregory Browne

"As gritty as the Detroit streets where it's set, DEAD WOOD grabs you early on and doesn't let go. As fine a a debut as you'll come across this year, maybe any year."

-author Tom Schreck

"Dan Ames is a sensation among readers who love fast-paced thrillers."

–Mystery Tribune

LONG SHOT

A John Rockne Mystery

by
Dan Ames

"The only real power comes out of a long rifle."
-*Joseph Stalin*

CHAPTER ONE

Nick Giordano had no idea what he was doing.

The sailboat had been a bit of an impulse purchase, he realized. It had belonged to another doctor who was leaving Michigan for a new gig in Colorado and since the boat hadn't been out of its slip in three years, he figured it would make more sense to sell it than to try to find a way to haul it out west.

So Nick had bought it cheap. Five grand. Which seemed like a good idea but then again he didn't really know anything about boats. He'd been on a few powerboats, failed miserably at water skiing and even gone fishing a few times. But he'd never really driven any of the boats. And while his sons both took sailing lessons at the Grosse Pointe Yacht Club, Nick had never taken any. Which made the purchase seem totally foolhardy.

An even worse idea was to take part in the weekly sailboat races at Windmill Pointe Park. Sure, it was a casual affair, mostly for fun. But here he was with a couple of buddies, trying to figure out which sails to use all while steering and drinking beer.

"No, the other way!" Nick's friend, a primary care physician named Doug Wendt, yelled. "You've got to go toward that buoy over there."

Nick spun the wheel, but the wind seemed to be pushing them out toward the center of Lake St. Clair into the shipping channel, which was never a good idea. At least there weren't any freighters around. That would be very, very bad.

"Reg, what the hell are you doing?" Nick yelled at his other friend, Claude Rieghels. Claude was Nick's partner in the medical practice and a renowned neurologist in his own right. When it came to sailing, however, he was usually put in charge of mixing martinis.

"I'm trying to trim this sail, Captain Ahab," Rieghels called back cheerfully. He knocked his bottle of beer over but caught it before it rolled off the deck into the water.

"Well, do it faster, Gilligan," Nick answered.

He looked ahead and saw the other sailboats way ahead of him and he was fairly confident they wouldn't even finish the course, let alone be a factor in the race. Now, they were all alone, several hundred yards away from the other boats.

It was one thing to be the head of neurology at a prestigious hospital like St. John's in Detroit, but it was quite another to be in the middle of Lake St. Clair with no idea how to get your sailboat going in the right direction.

But right then, Nick decided that he loved it. The fresh air. The sight of Canada on the other side of the lake. The spirit of friendly competition.

This was what it was all about. Not just having a sailboat, but getting out of the medical world for once, pausing in the endless race to make more money to buy more things. Just being out on the water, fresh air, and laughing with friends. He vowed then and there to do more of it, as often as he could.

Nick pictured his sons out here with him showing him

the ropes. Frederick was a fantastic sailor, Paul not so much. But Paul probably needed it more than his younger brother.

But for now, Nick was content to just enjoy being with his buddies, getting their collective ass kicked by more experienced boaters.

"Okay, I think I got it!" Rieghels called out. The sail caught the wind and the boat swung around, putting them parallel with the shoreline and in the same general direction as the other boats.

"All right!" Nick called out, shocked that his buddy had actually managed to do something right.

Nick stepped behind the wheel and never saw the bullet coming.

It entered his left temple and exited on the right, taking a good chunk of the neurologist's brain with it.

The force of the shot knocked him sideways and he fell to the deck, rolled off the boat into the water, leaving a smear of blood behind him.

CHAPTER TWO

There's bad acting, and then there's bad acting. Mitch Grovener had to be the worst actor I had ever seen in my life.

He had been collecting worker's compensation from his boss for nearly a year. The problem was, his boss was my client. And my client wasn't happy. He'd suspected the "accident" at the metal fabrication plant had been exaggerated to begin with. But when he started to hear rumors that his injured employee was telling friends about how much fish he was catching on Lake St. Clair, well, that had been the last straw.

Now, as I sat at my desk in my office looking over the surveillance photos of the "injured" worker, I had to laugh. The guy kept forgetting to put on his neck brace. And even when he did, he seemed to forget that he was supposed to be injured. Here he was with his neck brace, pushing his fishing boat into the water. Hey, here he is leaping off the boat onto the dock. Worst of all, here he is hauling a cooler full of beer back up to the house.

I opened up my official John Rockne Investigations email

account, attached the worst of the photos and fired them off to my client.

It would be up to him whether or not he wanted me to handle the confrontation, or his lawyers. The best bet would be for him to use his lawyers but if he asked me to, I would be happy to comply.

Nothing wrong with adding more billings.

I shut the computer down, locked up the office and headed home.

It was fall in Grosse Pointe and I always had the internal debate over whether my hometown was more beautiful in fall than spring. The towering trees, the beautiful homes, the spacious lawns, everything always looked great in fall.

But to be honest, I probably had to pick spring. Spring was all about the hope and joy of warmer temperatures. Of rebirth. Fall was all about getting ready for winter. And despite the fact that I'd spent all of my life in the Midwest, I'd never really become a big fan of winter.

Probably because the only thing I really liked about winter was watching football.

Fall wasn't bad, though, as long as I was able to ignore its meaning that winter was right around the corner.

Mentally blocking unpleasant realities was a talent of mine. They say that pessimists have a more accurate view of reality than optimists but with that comes a whole lot of unnecessary unpleasantness.

It only took me a few minutes to get from the village to my house. Home was a brick colonial with a nice yard and a seemingly endless parade of small jobs that only an old house could provide. Built in 1928, the house had great bones but required constant medical attention, if you get what I mean.

The good thing was, I could be very handy around the house. And by handy I mean I am very good at dialing my cell phone to hire people who can fix stuff.

Because I sure can't.

My skill is reprogramming the television's cable channel if the power ever goes out.

End of talent list.

I pulled up to the drive and saw a Grosse Pointe police car in front of my house. Ordinarily, that would set off alarm bells for most people. But the Chief of Police and I were very close.

As in, she's my sister.

The only thing that made me a little nervous was that my cell phone had died and I'd left both my regular charger and my car charger at home. Nothing pissed off my wife Anna more than when I did that, especially since she paid the household bills and hated how big the monthly cell phone had become. And then when she couldn't get ahold of me, the question of why we spent so much on cell phones typically came up. Not surprisingly.

I parked behind the squad car and entered the side door that opened onto a mud room and then a short flight of three steps into the kitchen.

The first thing I saw was my sister's gun, and then my wife, Anna, was standing in front of me, her face wet with tears.

My sister turned to me as well, giving me a look of dissatisfaction, probably because she'd tried to reach me on my cell, for whatever news I was about to receive.

"Someone shot Nick," Anna said, as she folded herself into my arms. I hugged her tight. Nick Giordano was her brother. I looked at Ellen, my sister. She nodded to me.

"He's dead, John," Anna said. "Someone killed him."

CHAPTER THREE

There was nothing to do but hold my wife, kiss away her tears and try to do everything I could to console her. Once she briefly stopped crying and went to the restroom, I ducked upstairs to check on the girls. They were doing their homework and I told them to keep at it. They didn't seem to be aware of what was going on downstairs.

When I came back down, Anna was on the phone.

I cracked open a bottle of wine and poured three glasses. I motioned to Anna that a glass was hers, and I took the other two into the living room where I found my sister sitting in a chair, scrolling through her cell phone.

"So tell me what the hell happened," I said and handed her a glass of wine.

I took a chair opposite her.

Ellen spoke softly. "He was on his boat with a couple of buddies doing the race at the park. They heard a shot, turned around, and he was gone. Went right over the side of the boat into the water. They fished him out, but he was dead.

"What the hell?" I asked. "Someone shot him from another boat?"

Ellen shook her head. "Don't think so. They were behind everyone else and from the angle he went overboard, he was shot by somebody from shore."

"You mean, with a rifle?"

"Had to have been. Would have been an impossible shot with a pistol. They were pretty far out."

"Holy shit," I said. "Are you sure it wasn't the guys on the boat?"

Ellen shook her head. "Obviously we haven't ruled anything out, but it doesn't seem likely. We tested both guys for gunshot residue and they were clean."

"That can be fooled," I said. Somewhere I thought I'd read you could beat the gunshot residue test with bleach.

"Thanks for the tip, Sherlock," Ellen said. She raised an eyebrow. This wasn't necessarily the best time for humor, but the Rockne clan had survived for many years on occasionally inappropriate behavior.

"Who's working the case?" I asked.

"Stocker and Radcliffe."

"Ugh," I said and rolled my eyes. Stocker was a little prick. The few times I'd been around him he always seemed to find a way to bring up my past and the incident that had gotten me kicked off the force.

"I met Nick once, didn't I?" Ellen asked me.

I searched my memory. "Yeah, I think you did. That one Christmas party we had a few years back. He was the tall guy with the glasses."

Ellen nodded.

Naturally, I knew Nick quite well. He was a great guy. Friendly, very welcoming when Anna married me and I got to know the Giordanos. As had been all of Anna's siblings.

"Anything else?" I asked, knowing it was a bit of a silly question.

"Nothing yet, John," she said, holding back from giving me another smart-ass reply.

"Man, this is bad," I said. One of the many reasons I had fallen in love with Anna Giordano was her love and commitment to family. She was a fierce defender of her family, as I had learned the hard way after making an innocent observation or two.

"Know anything about his wife and kids?" Ellen asked.

"Yeah," I said, thinking of his wife. Not exactly one of my favorite people in the world. "Katie. Two sons. Paul and Frederick. Paul is living in Chicago. Frederick lives downtown in a loft."

Ellen nodded. She didn't bother writing any of it down as her officers were sure to get the same information.

"Can you let me know what your team finds out?" I said.

She raised an eyebrow. "We'll see," she said. Cops didn't have a huge interest to fill in local private investigators on active cases and Ellen was no different.

Anna appeared in the doorway, her cell phone in her hand, held down against her leg. She had a look of confusion on her face as if she didn't know what to do.

She looked at me.

"We're going to need more wine," she said.

CHAPTER FOUR

They say that grief and anger are very close cousins and the next morning, Anna was a case in point. We had stayed up the night before and Anna had consumed more wine than I'd ever seen her drink before. In the morning, she was in pain both from the news of her brother, and the after effects.

But the grief I had seen so clearly was now being replaced with rage.

"Why the hell would anyone want to kill Nick?" she said. "He was a great doctor, good husband and father, and a smart businessman. His biggest vice was the occasional cigar."

I really wanted to be able to tell her something. Anything. But I had no information so I did what you were supposed to do; simply comfort her as best I could.

"Nick was the oldest and he could be a bully but when one of us was in trouble, he was always there for us," Anna said. "I used to have this bike I called 'Pinky' and one day, a neighborhood tough guy punched me in the stomach and took it. The next day, Nick came up the driveway wheeling Pinky and he had blood on his hands and shirt. It wasn't his own."

Anna barely got the last words out before she crumpled against me and began to sob. I stroked her beautiful hair and kissed the tears on her cheeks.

"Just give it time," I whispered. "Ellen will figure out what happened. She's the smart one in the family."

"You are too," Anna said. Her dark eyes were full of rage and hurt. "You need to figure out what happened, too."

Truth be told I was already planning on looking into it, but judging from Anna's intensity simply checking in on the official investigation wasn't going to be enough. I would have to tread carefully but I wanted to catch whoever was responsible for this just as much as Anna did.

"Your sister is great, and the police force is great, but they don't do many murders," she said. She visibly winced at the word, and then burst into tears.

I hugged my wife, and the girls came down the stairs. Anna wiped her face and hugged Isabel and then Nina. They were still sleepy so they didn't seem to notice anything. Telling them wasn't going to be easy. Anna had let me know she wanted to think about it before she told them.

My cell buzzed and I checked the screen. It was Ellen telling me to meet her at the lake and she gave me the cross streets, one of them being Lake Shore Drive which, not surprisingly, ran along the western edge of Lake St. Clair.

"That was Ellen, she wants me to meet her at a spot where she thinks the person may have been," I said, choosing my words carefully both for Anna's sake and the girls'.

"Okay," she said. "Will you be back soon? I have to meet everyone and go over arrangements."

"I should be back in an hour or two."

"Okay, that will work," she said, her voice soft and distant.

It absolutely ripped my heart apart to see the emotional state of my wife.

It also made me want to rip the heart out of the person who shot Nick Giordano.

CHAPTER FIVE

It wouldn't be much of a surprise to know that most of the homes in Grosse Pointe on Lakeshore Drive are of the mansion variety. Generally speaking, the smallest and least impressive home would still be worth several million dollars. The most expensive would probably clock in with an eight-figure price tag.

There are some giant, behemoth castles from which you might expect to see Prince William and Kate emerge skipping along with their kids and some finger sandwiches.

But there is variety. There are some new construction McMansions, some funky-looking homes from the fifties and sixties, and the occasional vacant lot.

When I say vacant lot, I'm not talking a weed-choked parcel where the local kids throw their garbage. I'm talking about a lot facing Lake St. Clair that would probably be worth about a million bucks all by itself.

Some of them even have landscaping.

The one that had a group of police cars parked in front of it was one of those.

I turned off of Lakeshore and parked just up the street,

away from the police cars. I had no desire to be accused of interfering. At least, not yet.

Ellen stood near the thickest part of the landscaping, a hedge that ran the entire width of the lot except for an opening off of Lakeshore. That's where if someone bought the lot and built a brand new mansion, they would put the entrance.

It occurred to me that the hedge was extremely thick and that the property bordering the lot in back was heavily wooded. If a shooter had positioned himself or herself in the thick bushes, there was a chance no one would have spotted him. Especially if the suspect had truly fashioned himself as a military type, he would have taken up his location earlier that day in the dark of morning and waited all day for the shot.

But it seemed absolutely ridiculous. Right here? On a busy street surrounded by multimillion-dollar homes? Not to mention, the sidewalk that ran along the road was a favorite of walkers, joggers and dog lovers. There was always traffic here, both vehicular and ambulatory.

What had the shooter done afterward?

As I approached the group, I saw Stocker turn and look at me and then make an exaggerated eye roll. He was a weird little guy. Short, slightly bow-legged, with hair that was just a little too long.

But he had bright, intelligent eyes. Blue. And I'd heard that he was a smart bastard.

His partner, Radcliffe, was a guy with prematurely gray hair and a black mustache. He nodded at me.

"Who called the B-team?" Stocker mumbled and then shot a glance at Ellen to see if she'd heard. She had, but you never would have guessed it.

"Do another canvass, see if they're home yet," Ellen said to Radcliffe and she gestured at the property behind the vacant lot.

She left Stocker standing there and walked toward me and then past me. I followed.

We walked to her squad car and she stopped to let a jogger run by.

"This is a strange one," she said.

"The shooter was here?" I said, glancing around the very definition of Grosse Pointe.

"Too early to tell, but someone was in there recently. We should be able to get a partial footprint. No shell casings."

She pointed out toward the lake. "But that's right about where your brother-in-law was shot." She made a gesture from the spot on the lake following a direct line to the hedge behind us. "The forensic guys did their best, based on the boat's GPS to get a fix on exactly where they were in the water. And then based on the statements from the two guys on the boat, he was at the helm, looking straight ahead."

Running the logic through my mind I had a million questions.

"I know you've got a ton of questions but that's all I'm giving you," Ellen said. "And you know that this is just a theory. A guess, right now. But since I know Anna I want to help." A small smile tugged at the corner of her mouth.

"Unfortunately that means helping you a little bit, too."

Before I could answer, Ellen walked to her car.

"Why don't you go work on Stocker," she said. "He clearly hasn't bought into your charm yet."

She slammed the door and pulled out onto Lakeshore.

I glanced over my shoulder.

Stocker had a legal pad in one hand and his cell phone in the other.

There was no point in approaching him.

Besides, Anna needed me back home.

CHAPTER SIX

The next two days were a whirlwind. The hardest part was sitting down with Nina and Isabel to tell them that Uncle Nick had gone to a better place. It was difficult for Anna who did her best not to shock the girls with an onslaught of tears.

At the visitation, the first person I saw was Nick's wife, Katie. She was a short woman, verging on chunky, who had thinning hair and chalky skin.

I did my best to set aside any past issues between us and I went to hug her. She stepped back and offered her hand for me to shake, which I did.

"I'm so sorry," I said. She gave me a highly perfunctory smile and moved immediately to the girls and Anna.

Nick's sons, Paul and Frederick were there as well. I offered my condolences and was shocked at how much older they seemed.

Paul, the eldest, was a mirror image of his father. He had a powerful build, brown eyes, and the olive skin so many of the Giordano family had, including Anna.

Frederick was Paul's complete opposite: tall and thin with blonde hair and blue eyes.

The rest of Anna's siblings were all there, too. She had two sisters and two brothers, all who lived out of state, and her parents had flown in from Florida.

I did my best to keep an eye on Anna, to make sure I was there for her if she needed a break, and to also be in charge of Nina and Isabel.

The day bled into the next and that one into the next as the proceedings came to an end and Anna's siblings and parents all flew back to their respective cities.

Finally, a full week after Nick's murder, Anna and I were back at home. The girls were upstairs in bed, and it was a Sunday night. Which meant tomorrow everything would go back to normal, understanding that nothing would ever be normal again for Anna.

But the Monday routine would come back and I hoped that in some sense that would provide a relief to Anna. I understood the entire process was meant to aid in grieving, but I was glad that she would now be able to spend less time thinking about what had happened to her brother.

Of course, I couldn't have been more wrong.

"What else are you working on?" Anna asked me. We were sitting at the kitchen table. She had a grocery list in front of her, as well as a list of other things she needed to do this week.

"I wrapped up the workers comp case and invoiced my client, so that check should be coming in," I said. "I've got a guy who jumped bail but I know where he is, I just have to lead my client to him who will do the rest."

When I looked up, I could see Anna was not happy with my answer.

As quickly as I could, I added, "And I asked Ellen to swing by my office so we could chat about Nick's case without prying eyes. You know, a police station is like a junior high school when it comes to gossip."

The look of anger passed from Anna's eyes and she nodded.

"I want you to find out who killed Nick," she said. "I want that bastard to fry."

CHAPTER SEVEN

The police tape was still there, but it was easy to duck under. Still, I had no intention of being spotted by Stocker and then accused of disturbing an active crime scene, so I tread carefully around the ground.

If this was where the shooter had been, it was a good spot, I had to grudgingly admit. The landscaping was deep enough that he could have completely hidden his body and certainly his rifle would have been concealed as well. I thought of the footage I'd seen of American snipers in Iraq and how they would set up on a rooftop, shooting through a hole in the wall.

Could this shooter have done that? Did he target Nick specifically or was he just looking to shoot someone on a boat and my brother-in-law had sailed directly into his sights.

I made a mental note to track down someone who would know more about guns than I did, not a challenging feat to be honest.

But it made me wonder if the rifle was fixed wouldn't that mean he had somewhat limited movement? So he couldn't have turned forty-five degrees to the left or right to shoot. It would have have been pretty much a straight shot.

And how had the shooter chosen this spot? Was he a local Grosse Pointer? Had he jogged past this parcel? Driven past it? Did he own a house nearby?

If he owned a house nearby he had vast financial means, that was certain.

My cell phone buzzed and I saw it was my best friend and intrepid reporter, Nate Becker. I'd known Nate my whole life and for years he'd been a reporter for the local paper before taking a job at the Free Press downtown.

He'd already called to offer myself and Anna condolences, but this time it was all business.

"Any progress?" he asked.

"None yet," I said. "How about you? Any scuttlebutt?"

It may have seemed like a strange question, but the fact was murders in Grosse Pointe were rare. Unlike its next-door neighbor Detroit, which usually finished in the top three for highest murder rates of American cities, my community was much more used to petty crimes. Outright murder in Grosse Pointe wasn't all that common.

So the killing of a fairly well-known Grosse Pointe doctor, most likely shot with a long-range rifle while racing on his sailboat was making the rounds of Detroit as well. It had even made some national news sites.

"Nothing much," he said. "I've got all my sources keeping an ear out, though. You'll be the first call I make if I learn anything new."

We agreed to meet for a drink later in the week and I was about to put my phone away when I got a text from Ellen.

It simply said: *Good news, bad news. Found bullet. A .223.*

And that was it.

I knew enough about guns to realize why she said the fact that the bullet was a .223 caliber was bad news. It was one of the most common rifle cartridges used. It was a common round for the military as well as Average Joe deer hunters and kids going out to the woods to blast squirrels.

There was nothing special about a .223.

Slipping the phone into my pocket, I got back into my car and drove around the block, which was a bit of a misnomer. The blocks here were huge and not square. So in order to get to the houses surrounding the parcel, I had to make several twists and turns. In short, I learned nothing, other than there were even more big, beautiful houses in this area than I had dreamed.

With a sigh, I realized what I had to do. Whenever a married person is murdered, the first suspicion cast is always on the spouse. And although Katie Giordano was not my favorite person in the world, I needed to talk to her. For two reasons. One, to get a feel for the possibility that something had been going on with Nick that only a wife would know. And two, try to help her. She was still family, after all.

But I had a feeling the meeting would not go well.

CHAPTER EIGHT

As befitting a successful doctor in Grosse Pointe, Nick Giordano owned a beautiful, expansive Tudor a half a block from Lake St. Clair.

It was a stunningly beautiful house with a slate roof, thick wooden beams and gorgeous windows with thick, leaded glass.

I parked on the street, went to the front door and rang the bell. After a few moments, the door opened and I came face to face with Katie Giordano.

"Oh," she said, and looked over my shoulder, probably hoping to get a glimpse of Anna or the girls.

But it was just me.

Her expression reflected her obvious disappointment.

"Hi Katie, I'm wondering if I could come in and chat with you for a few minutes." I tried to keep my voice as even as possible. The woman's husband had been murdered, after all. Knowing how relieved I felt that Anna had at least put the funeral behind her and was beginning, perhaps, to move on to the next stage of grief, I felt a pang of guilt about having to talk to Katie.

But my loyalties were to my wife, and talking to Nick's widow was essential to figuring out who may have wanted to hurt him.

She stepped aside and I walked past her, catching a strong whiff of alcohol. Probably wine. Nick had supposedly sent Katie off to Napa Valley for some kind of wine tour that had turned into something more. The family grapevine, no pun intended, had suggested that Katie may have developed a bit of a problem with wine.

Some people in the family figured Nick had encouraged the trip to Napa as a way for him to avoid her, or it was a way for her to indulge in her apparently increasing love of alcohol.

"Something to drink?" she said, her voice utterly devoid of enthusiasm. I stepped inside and closed the door behind me.

"No thank you," I said.

She walked through a hallway that reminded me of a European grotto, whatever that was. The floor was hardwood, but the walls seemed to be a textured marble of some sort and the short hallway opened out onto a great room with the kitchen to the left and a huge living area to the right.

Katie went to the kitchen's island where there was a glass of red wine the size of a fish bowl.

I looked back at the living space.

"Are you moving?" I asked, looking at the stacks and stacks of boxes that pretty much filled the area. There were small walkways to a large leather couch, a television and a bookshelf.

"No, why do you ask?"

I looked again at the boxes and saw they were unopened packages from stores. Nordstrom. Pottery Barn. Crate & Barrel.

Holy shit.

There had been rumors that Nick was having a problem

with Katie's spending, that she was ordering stuff from catalogs night and day.

It looked to me like those rumors were true.

Before I could answer, she cut me off.

"What did you want to talk about?" she asked, sounding
like she was asking a dentist how long the root canal was
going to take. She took a long drink from her wineglass and
smacked her lips afterward.

"Well, I want to help find out who is responsible for what
happened."

"But you're not a cop anymore," she snapped at me. "And
when you were a cop…"

She purposely let the comment hang and I, of course,
understood what she was getting at. I had made a horrible
mistake, one that resulted in an innocent young man being
murdered. It was why I had been kicked off the force.

"Right, but I do a fair amount of investigating–"

"Like cheating spouses and insurance scams, right?" she
said. Another long drink of wine. She glanced over at the
kitchen table where there were more catalogs. I got the
feeling I was keeping her from her shopping.

It irked me that her tone had taken on an even greater
sound of extreme condescension. She took yet another long
drink from her wineglass and peered at me over its rim.

"Among other things," I said. "Do you have any idea who
might have wanted to hurt Nick?"

"Look, I've been through this with the real cops," she
answered. "I certainly don't feel like talking about it now.
With you."

Katie opened up a catalog, this one from a jewelry store
and began flipping through the pages. I could see pages of
diamond rings and necklaces.

"Okay, well, if I learn anything of use I'll let you know," I said. "And if you think of anything and need me to look into it, just let me know, I'd like to help in any way I can."

Her phone rang and she picked it up. Before she answered, she looked at me and gave me a nod toward the door.

I let myself out.

CHAPTER NINE

Contacting Frederick was easy. Anna had his cell phone number because she'd had to pick him up one time from the airport as a favor to Nick and the number was still in her contact information.

So I called Frederick who wasn't able to talk on the phone but said he could meet me for a quick cup of coffee when he took a break from work.

One of the draws of downtown Detroit for young people is the availability of cheap condos. However, there's more to them than just the price. The condos are much bigger and nicer than their ilk in other cities for the price.

Frederick's building was in yet another funky neighborhood of Detroit, a few rehabbed buildings that were attracting young people, side-by-side with abandoned homes and the occasional drug dealer on the corner.

We met at a coffee shop full of hipsters. The uniform was flannel and beards. And those were the women.

Upon seeing Frederick, it struck me again how he looked nothing like anyone else in his family. While the Giordanos tended to have dark hair, dark eyes and a thick musculature,

Frederick's tall thin frame, combined with blond hair and blue eyes always struck me as such an anomaly.

He smiled when he saw me, got up and shook my hand.

"Uncle John," he said.

I bought him a cup of foamy something or other and I got a black coffee.

It was good.

Say what you might about these hipsters, they could brew a damn fine cup of joe.

"How are you holding up, Frederick?" I asked. He went by Frederick. It was never shortened to Fred or Freddie. The name fit him perfectly.

"Fine, I guess," he said. He looked a little tired, but other than that, normal. He started to say something else but then stopped himself. Probably to keep his emotions in check and to not start crying in public. Grieving is good, but at some point you have to try to compartmentalize it, and I had a feeling that's what he was trying to do.

Which didn't make my job any easier.

"You know my sister Ellen and her team are doing everything they can to find the person responsible," I said.

Frederick nodded. "I've offered to help her in any way I can," he said.

A pair of middle-aged women came into the coffee shop, hesitated and then went to the counter. A couple of North Shore Nancys out on a coffee adventure.

"So I have to ask," I continued. "Was there anyone or anything you can think of that might have had something to do with this?"

Frederick let out a sigh. "No. That's just it. Paul and I have talked repeatedly since...it happened. And there's just nothing. You know, my Dad worked. He worked all the time."

I did know that. Anna had occasionally mentioned how Nick was never at home, that his medical practice took up his entire life and he was always rushing from office to office, rarely returned her phone calls and was usually a no-show at any family functions.

"It had slowed down a little bit once we left home, from what I gather," Frederick continued. "There was the sailboat. And I guess he had started golfing a little bit in the summer."

It seemed a little odd to me that Nick would wait until the boys were out of the house to start taking some time off from work, but maybe that was just a coincidence.

"Once my Mom got better, that kind of changed things, too," he ventured.

Katie had been diagnosed with cancer a few years back. They had caught it very early, though, and with aggressive treatment it had gone into remission and she'd been cancer-free for years, as I understood it.

"It took a while for things to go back to normal, though," he added.

I was about to let that go by, but there was something about the way he said it that made me wonder. Whenever anyone is diagnosed with cancer it's a game-changer and sure, it would take time for things to go back to normal even if the patient survived.

But there was something about the way he said it.

"Is that because of the severity of her illness?" I tentatively asked.

Frederick shrugged and I could tell he was debating whether or not to add anything. Luckily, he did.

"My Mom and her sister are big believers in alternative medicine," he finally said.

How odd, I thought. To be married to a doctor and not believe in what he practices.

"That would seem to be a conflict," I ventured.

"It was," Frederick said. "She wanted Dad to spend a ton of money on all kinds of weird stuff. A bunch of bizarre treatments that had nothing to do with medicine. Or science. Or reality, for that matter."

He glanced up as a man in a suit with a bowler walked into the coffee shop. Hipster coffee shops attract all kinds.

"But Dad was a real doctor. A great doctor. And even though he would have done anything to help her get better, there was no way he was going to waste money on a bunch of quacks. And it wasn't about the money. He just refused to do it as a practitioner of real medicine."

His voice got a little shaky.

"That makes sense," I said. "It would be like asking an atheist to donate money to a church."

"He refused to do it," Frederick said. "And Mom never forgave him for that."

"But she got better," I pointed out.

"Yeah, he was right, of course. It was the traditional stuff that got her better. Surgery and chemo. Not some kind of California mud bath and seaweed diet."

"Of course."

"Things were never quite the same after that around the house, though," Frederick said.

I wondered if that had anything to do with the shitload of new mail-order packages that filled the living room at the Giordano house. Or the rumors of excess drinking.

"But my Dad was successful and money was never a problem," Frederick said. "In fact, he said the future never looked brighter and that's why he was able to buy the sailboat and start taking some time off."

Frederick shrugged. "I wish he'd been able to do that when we were growing up, though. We hardly ever saw him."

There wasn't much I could say to that so I just nodded.

The rest of it made a lot of sense to me. Katie was pissed off that Nick didn't agree to pay for the quack medicine stuff so she got even by going crazy with spending money elsewhere.

"How is Paul doing?" I asked, to change the subject slightly.

"Happy to be back in Chicago," Frederick said. "It would be nice to get away for awhile. I'm probably going to go visit him in a couple of weeks."

"That's a great idea. How is the start-up going?" I knew Frederick had been an extremely skilled computer programmer and had launched several companies in Detroit.

It probably sounded odd to the outsider, but Detroit had actually exploded recently with tech firms moving in, thanks in part to a mega high-speed data system being installed by one of the companies downtown. That, in addition to the cheap real estate and significant tax breaks.

"Really well," Frederick said. "One of our apps is getting a lot of attention from Facebook. There have been rumors of an offer coming, but we'll see," he said.

"What's an app?" I asked. And then we both laughed. I knew what an app was after all. It was short for application, as in job application. Right?

We finished our coffees and briefly talked about other stuff. He asked about Isabel and Nina, listened to my stories of their goofiness with genuine enjoyment. I liked Frederick. He was an incredibly intelligent young man, and although a bit standoffish at times, he was polite and seemed honestly interested in other people.

So why did I get the feeling that deep down something was wrong with him?

CHAPTER TEN

When I got Nick's other son, Paul, on the phone, I asked him the same questions I asked Frederick and I got the exact same answers.

Paul had always been the extrovert while Frederick was more quiet and internally focused. Anna had told me some stories about Paul's high school days which sounded like they consisted of quite a bit of partying and fraternizing with the opposite sex.

It wouldn't have been a surprise for me to learn that Paul had been the ladies' man. He had the best of the Giordano looks.

We chatted briefly and he confirmed most of what Frederick had said, never seeming to be caught off guard.

After we finished talking I headed to my office.

Main Street in Grosse Pointe is actually a street called Kercheval. And the downtown is simply called the Village. There's a second village just down from the first one called The Hill.

My office is in the Village, above a jewelry store and next to a Merrill Lynch brokerage office. I've always said that if business goes sour, I'll just drill a hole in the floor and rob the jewelry store. Do a kind of Mission Impossible thing where I dangle from the ceiling.

Yeah, right.

I unlocked the door to my office, walked through my little waiting area that had a couple of chairs, a table with some various law enforcement magazines strategically scattered about, and a nautical print on the wall. It was a sailboat making its way through rough seas with a storm on the horizon. I liked to think that my potential clients could relate.

It felt weird to boot up my computer and start cyber stalking my deceased brother-in-law. But I figured it was something I had to do even though I also knew Ellen and her team were already scouring every possible lead. But it also occurred to me that most of the time my clients were complete strangers and now I knew the deceased pretty well. It would expedite my searching, at least that's what I was going to go with.

The first sets of listings all had to do with his medical practice. The next grouping consisted of social obligations in which he had donated some money to some charity or Grosse Pointe institution. I was about to give up when near the end of the Google search results I spotted a listing about his sailboat and prior race results.

That was interesting.

The first thing Ellen would be trying to figure out is if the murder was random, or of Nick Giordano had been the target. And if he was the target, how had the killer known where he would be? Seeing the prior race results in black-and-white at least confirmed to me that he had been doing this for some time.

So if a killer had wanted to set up a shot, it would have been easy. The racecourse was always the same. Everyone knew that, and most likely the killer would have, too. He just would have had to find his shooting spot and wait for Nick to sail into his sights.

But is that what really happened?

Or had the shooter simply waited for *anyone* to sail into his kill zone?

That was the million-dollar question.

CHAPTER ELEVEN

"Are you napping?" Ellen's voice spoke to me from my cell phone. I glanced at the clock on the wall. It was just past eleven in the morning.

"Cute," I said. "Are you just getting into work?"

"Been here since seven," she replied. "You were probably drooling into your pillow."

I sighed.

"Can I help you?" I said. "Psychologically speaking?"

"I already told you about the shooter using .223 ammo, right?"

"Yep," I answered. .223 ammo was the equivalent of McDonalds – tons of them everywhere, nearly impossible to trace.

"I don't know why I'm telling you the latest news, probably because Anna is the closest thing I have to family here in Grosse Pointe," Ellen said.

That was a good one, I had to admit.

"Ballistics matched the rounds to a cold case," she continued.

"You're kidding me," I said.

"Nope. Victim was a woman named Colleen Fairbanks. Lived in Bloomfield Hills. Married, no children. Worked in finance. They took a long look at her husband, but he was in California at the time."

"When and where?"

"Six months or so back," Ellen answered. "In a park north of the city known for its hiking trails. She was alone at the time, except for her dog. Apparently she hiked the park frequently for exercise."

"Easy for a shooter to set up, then," I pointed out.

"Very easy."

"What's the husband's story?" I asked.

"Brian Fairbanks," Ellen said. "Car guy, but not for the Big Three. He's involved in electric vehicles."

"Huh."

"That's all I got," Ellen said. "Which is way more than you deserve, frankly. Because this really ought to be a two-way street, but I feel like you've got nothing, as usual."

"Thanks, as always for your support," I said. "But actually, I do have some things to share."

It took me a few minutes to fill her in on what I'd learned from Katie Giordano, as well as Frederick.

"Interesting, but nothing really to go on," she said.

"That's what I figured," I said. "Anything else for me? Or is that all you've *really* got?" I asked, figuring she probably wasn't going to tell me *everything*.

Her response?

A dial tone.

CHAPTER TWELVE

The newspapers told me everything and nothing.

Colleen Fairbanks had been murdered. Shot to death while hiking a nature trail not far from her home in Bloomfield Hills.

A single shot to the head.

From a long distance.

So did we have a sniper on the loose like the two maniacs in Washington, D.C. a few years ago? The guys who had customized the trunk of their car so they could shoot without being seen?

The Colleen Fairbanks investigation had apparently fizzled out before it even really got started.

There had been virtually no evidence.

No leads.

No suspects.

Now a cold case.

That is, until Nick Giordano had been shot with the same gun.

The husband had an airtight alibi. Still, I knew that in cases like this the husband was always under suspicion. He may have had an alibi at the time, but he was still the husband and whenever there was a married woman murdered with no sign of a clear suspect, a dark cloud of suspicion immediately hovered over the husband.

Usually until the case was solved or he died. And even if he died, the whispers never did.

The husband.

Brian Fairbanks. I continued to surf the Internet for more information. There were a lot of articles about him. A self-made millionaire with a passion for the environment and green engineering. He'd worked in the stock market, eventually buying his way into numerous green companies before finally starting his own.

Fairbanks Automotive.

A leading firm in the design and production of electric cars.

I called Nate.

"Colleen Fairbanks," I said.

"Wow, that's a blast from the recent past," he said. "So to speak."

"Murdered from a long distance," I pointed out.

I could almost sense Nate's reporter excitement vibrating through the line. I had to be careful, though. I didn't want to spill the beans that my sister had entrusted to me. That would be bad. Very bad.

"So there's a connection to Nick Giordano?" he asked.

"Not that I can really prove," I said, which was true. My sister probably could, along with the Grosse Pointe Police Department, but I, John Rockne, couldn't.

Nate was my best friend in the world, but Ellen was my sister.

"Okay," he said, the disappointment evident in his voice. "That Fairbanks case is probably still active, but the file is on the back burner I'm sure."

"Do you know the guy in charge of the back burner cases?" I asked. "I'd love to see if there's any connection between Colleen Fairbanks and my brother-in-law. You know," I added. "A literal connection, not just a guess."

Which, of course, was my way of telling Nate that the cases were connected, probably through forensics, but there had to be more to the story. And there was no phrase more beloved by reporters than 'there was more to the story.'

Nate and I agreed to meet for lunch at Green Dot Stables, a Detroit eatery and fine tradition downtown. Lots of sliders. Gourmet sliders. I'd seen Nate put away nearly two dozen in one sitting. I would have to bring my credit card. I didn't have that much cash.

After I disconnected with Nate I went back to the Internet and looked at some photos of Colleen Fairbanks.

She was a looker. A short, modern haircut with blue eyes and a face that featured perfect lines. I knew the minute I saw her face that she had probably never taken a bad picture in her life.

It gave me a thought that I immediately felt guilty for having. But I thought of the train wreck of a woman I'd talked to at Nick's house. Katie. His wife.

And then I looked again at a photo of Colleen Fairbanks.

No comparison.

I wondered if Nick had felt the same way.

CHAPTER THIRTEEN

By now, they knew about the Fairbanks woman.

He smiled at the thought of her. It hadn't been the first person he'd ever killed. But it had been the first person he'd killed for reasons other than pleasure.

A small laugh escaped his thin, cruel lips. It wasn't like he was Ted Bundy or something. Christ, no. The first one had been in college, a little rough sex that got out of hand, fueled mostly by booze and coke. Luckily, she'd been a stripper that worked part-time as a hooker, so he'd dumped the body and no one had ever been the wiser.

The second one hadn't really been his fault. He'd drugged a friend's mom because she was extremely hot. After he'd had his fun with her, he noticed she'd stopped breathing. Luckily, she was a typical Grosse Pointe woman. Married to a wealthy man who never gave her the time of day so she whiled away the hours with booze, prescription drugs, and flirting with her son's friends.

Luckily, her husband had covered up the death as an accidental overdose.

But those had been earlier in his life. Still, he'd realized that murder didn't scare him. He always knew he would probably kill *again, when the time was right and the opportunity was too good to pass up.*

So when the stars aligned and he realized that Colleen Fairbanks was going to have to be eliminated, he'd worked tirelessly to put together a plan.

His endless and secret fascination with guns had paid off.

Of course, he knew the best way to murder someone was to make it look like it wasn't a murder at all. He'd learned that with his friend's mom.

But try as he did, he couldn't come up with a way to do it. So the next best thing was to kill her and simply leave no evidence. Or, more accurately, only leave the evidence he wanted to leave.

Now, as he sat in his den and studied the rifle on the wall, he thought about how excited he was to use it again.

It would be soon.

Very soon.

CHAPTER FOURTEEN

Timelines are essential. It's like the five w's of reporting. Who, what, where, why and when.

So I knew who was murdered. I knew where. I knew when. The only one I didn't know was why. Of course, if I knew why, the case would be solved.

For now, I would have to focus on when and what the timeline might or might not mean.

There was no doubt on when Nick had been murdered, so I decided to take a look at the exact time Colleen Fairbanks had been gunned down and see if that would tell me anything.

A quick search confirmed what Ellen had told me, that Colleen Fairbanks had been murdered nearly six months earlier. Six months would have been a long time for Nick to have dealt with her murder, if he knew her, that is.

If Nick had been involved with Colleen Fairbanks in some way, he would have certainly known about her death. For one thing, it had been in all of the newspapers and probably on the television news as well. So if he had an idea of who she was, there would have been plenty of opportunity for him to get wind of what had happened.

Additionally, if he had been involved with Colleen Fair-banks, it stood to reason that he would have most likely done some investigating, or if nothing else, he would have talked to someone about it.

But who?

I had learned enough at this point to guess with a fair amount of confidence that it wouldn't have been his wife. Not unless he wanted to have his ass handed to him. Or another few thousand dollars of catalog merchandise charged to his platinum American Express.

One question was, if he was involved with Colleen Fair-banks and she was a venture capitalist or startup investor, would it have been a business relationship? In which case Nick's partner ought to have known about it.

I had delayed talking to him until now, wanting something more than just a bunch of questions that were little more than stabs in the dark.

What I did know was that Nick and his business partner were at least friends on some level outside of the medical practice. After all, Nick's partner had been on the boat when Nick had been murdered.

It took me a minute to lock up the office, get into the car, and hop onto Cadieux Road headed toward the freeway. At the first spotlight I checked my rearview mirror and saw a black Chevy Impala behind me. Something triggered a flutter in my brain. Where had I seen that car before? And what was the deal with the face behind the steering wheel? It, too, looked familiar.

The Impala followed me all the way to the freeway but when I turned onto the ramp to merge, I lost sight of the car. But not before I caught a quick glimpse of the face of the driver behind the wheel.

It was a woman's face. She had short, spiked blonde hair and wore sunglasses.

Grosse Pointe was essentially a small town, so when I saw the woman's face, I didn't really give it another thought. Because here, if you didn't know someone, you certainly knew someone who did. And even if you didn't recognize a person right away, that didn't mean that you had actually never met them. Because the odds were fairly good that you probably had bumped into them at some point, if you'd lived in Grosse Pointe long enough.

So seeing vaguely familiar faces happened all the time. Especially with the constant number of parties going on every weekend, it seemed. Parents of fellow elementary students, sports parents, neighborhood block parties, the small cluster of bars and restaurants that everyone frequented. Plus, the one thing nearly all Grosse Pointers loved to do was drink.

So I promptly filed the face of the spiky blonde-haired woman away, for now.

But something about that face bothered me.

CHAPTER FIFTEEN

Michigan Neurological Services had multiple offices but the main one was located at Harper Avenue and Fifteen Mile Road. The parking lot was crowded and there was a huge semi-trailer parked to the right of the modern, single story office building. There was a sign on the side of the trailer that read Magnetic Resonance Imaging.

Really? An MRI in a semi-trailer?

I shrugged my shoulders. I'd seen Nick Giordano's house. He had made himself a pretty penny so I wasn't about to become some kind of Judgey Judgerton.

I parked, went inside and asked to see Dr. Claude Rieghels. The extremely attractive receptionist – think young Sophia Loren meets young Raquel Welch joined for a three-some by Mary Ann from Gilligan's Island - asked me if I had an appointment or wished to make one.

I wasn't really sure exactly what she said as I was still semi-lost in my ridiculous reverie. Eventually, though, her words got through to me.

"No, I don't have an appointment, but my name is John Rockne and I'm a member of Dr. Giordano's family and I'm investigating his murder," I answered. "So I do need to speak to Dr. Rieghels as it's very important."

"Ok, let me see what I can do," she answered.

There was a stack of files to the left of the reception desk and I pretended to be intrigued by them while Sophia-Raquel-Mary Ann spoke to someone on the other end of the line.

Moments later, a nurse appeared in the doorway to my right.

"Sir? You can come with me, please."

With a quick thank you to Sophia-Raquel-Mary Ann I followed the nurse down the hallway to Dr. Rieghels' office.

"He's with a patient but he will be able to see you in five or ten minutes."

After she left, I took a look around the doctor's office. It was what you'd expect. There were pictures on the desk of a family. The wife was a trophy blonde, two strapping sons, one in a football uniform. And two framed diplomas. One from the University of Michigan. The other from Emory University in Atlanta.

Color me impressed.

The medical books on his bookshelf were also to be expected and I was slowly making my way through the titles when the door opened and Dr. Rieghels stepped inside.

He was a short, barrel of a man with a bald head and a spring in his step. He wore a white coat with a stethoscope around his neck, tan slacks and loafers with tassels.

"How can I help you?" he asked, in a tone of voice that actually made me believe he wanted to help.

"John Rockne," I said, sticking my hand out. "I'm married to Anna Giordano, Nick's sister."

He smiled. "I think we met once, maybe at the office Christmas party."

See what I mean?

"Obviously, I'm here to talk to you about Nick's murder," I said. "Had he done anything differently before his death? Noticed any changes with him? Anything unusual?"

Rieghels shook his head. "No, not at all." Rieghels rubbed his forehead. "Nick was a fantastic doctor and an even better person. I can't believe this happened."

I waited for the doctor to regain his composure.

"Does the name Colleen Fairbanks ring any bells?" I finally asked.

He frowned and then shook his head again. "I don't think so. The name I might have heard somewhere before but I can't place it. But I'm positive I don't know her. Why?"

"Just a lead I'm following up on," I answered. "How was Nick's relationship at home?"

I kind of already knew the answer, but I was curious to see how he would react.

It was obvious that he had visibly tensed at the bluntness of the question.

"Nick and I didn't really get into our personal lives," he said, which was a pretty even response. It was also an obvious lie. But not all lies are told with malicious intent. And I got the feeling that Rieghels was putting down some bullshit to protect his dead friend. Or his dead friend's family.

"But you did sail together sometimes," I followed up, not wanting to totally let him off the hook.

"Sure," he admitted. "Once a month in the race but that was a new thing. We didn't really know what the hell we were doing." He smiled at the memory. I got the distinct feeling that he had really enjoyed Nick Giordano's company.

"So Nick hadn't been sailing long, then?"

Rieghels shrugged. "Maybe. I don't know. All I know is that I had absolutely no idea what I was doing. All of my boating experience had been with boats that had motors. Big motors. I had no idea how sails worked, or how to tie them off. He usually put me in charge of cocktails."

A silence followed before I asked, "How is the business doing?"

"Couldn't be better. We'd recently expanded adding another office. But we had decided that was it," he held up his hands as if to stop an avalanche. "We all work enough hours and any more expanding would mean that I would never be home at all. Just work around the clock. That isn't worth it to me. It wasn't worth it to Nick, either."

I thought that point might be open for debate, but I left it at that.

"I talked to Nick's son, Frederick," I said. "He told me that he thought his Dad was actually working less. That he seemed to be doing a few more things outside of the office. Does that sound right?"

Dr. Rieghels contemplated the question. "Possibly," he said, rocking back and forth slightly in his chair. "But Nick was really the brains behind the whole practice. I know that he had cut back on seeing patients, but he did the bulk of the administrative work. Finding the buildings. Hiring other docs, managing payments and revenue. So I know he was in the office way less than he'd ever been, but that doesn't neces-sarily mean he was working less, if you know what I mean."

It did make sense to me. As a small business owner myself, I understood the difference between doing the work and running the company.

We talked a little more but I learned nothing of impor-tance so I thanked Dr. Rieghels, left the office and got into the car.

When I pulled onto Harper and headed for the freeway, I checked my rearview mirror.

A black Impala was behind me, driven by a woman with spiked blonde hair.

CHAPTER SIXTEEN

Since Frederick was here in Detroit and Paul was in Chicago, I decided to take the easy way out and call the son closest to home, just in case I had to follow up in person.

He answered right away and I asked him if he had ever heard of a woman named Colleen Fairbanks.

"Doesn't sound familiar," he said. "Why?"

"Just following up on a lead," I answered. "Probably nothing."

"Do you think my Dad knew her?" he asked.

"It's a possibility."

"Would this have been before or after my Mom's trip to Napa?"

The first thing I considered was the timeline of when Nick may or may not have been involved with Colleen Fairbanks and immediately after that it struck me what his question meant.

"That was a wine-tasting trip to Napa, right?" I asked, stalling for time as I tried to figure out a way to get more information.

"Yeah, I guess," he said, with little to no conviction.

Before I could get another question in, he cut me off.

"Look, I have to go, okay?" he said, his voice anxious. And I felt bad. I knew the kid, even though he was now a young man. He was a good guy and the last thing I'd meant to do was to badger him into revealing information he didn't want to.

But there was still a killer out there, and I had promised my wife I would do everything I possibly could to catch him.

I tried to ask a follow-up question but I heard the sound of him disconnecting. My cell phone screen showed the call was over.

That was weird, I thought.

Why had Frederick seemed so agitated about the issue of Katie going out to Napa for some wine tasting? Hell, Anna and I had done that while we were engaged.

The problem was, I hated wine.

My memory of Napa was Anna getting pissed off every time I asked the winery people if they had any beer around.

The bigger question, as I pondered Frederick's response, was did I believe him about his Dad not knowing Colleen Fairbanks?

Somewhere in my notes would be Dr. Claude Rieghels' phone. I called him and left a voicemail inquiring whether or not he could check to see if Colleen Fairbanks had done any business with the medical practice.

Something told me it wasn't going to be that easy.

CHAPTER SEVENTEEN

Back in my office, I popped open the fridge and helped myself to a bottle of Point beer. The memory of all that crappy wine in Napa had made me thirsty. In fact, why didn't they call it Crappy Valley, because that wine was terrible.

I'm kidding, of course. Sort of.

Point beer, however, was the good stuff. It was my favorite beer, brewed in north central Wisconsin. The nearest place I could buy it was at a gourmet grocery store in Lansing, so I had to make the hour drive occasionally to stock up on my supply.

I twisted off the cap and took a long drink. A coffee might have been a better idea but I figured I was closer to the cocktail hour and further away from the caffeine-cutoff hour to merit my choice.

Besides, the beer tasted pretty damn good. As always.

My cell phone rang and I saw Nate's name in the display.

"You must have some good news if you're not waiting until our lunch to spring it on me," I said into the phone.

"Don't know if it's good or bad," he answered. "Besides, as

a reporter I don't really believe in either. News is just news, John."

"Thank you, Professor Becker."

"What I can tell you is that Colleen Fairbanks was a very successful investor," he said. I heard the sound of paper shuffling and could picture him digging through his notes at his desk. "She'd managed money for quite some time before branching out into the venture capital arena. And she did really well there."

I put down the beer and inspired by the sound of his notes, decided to start taking my own.

"How well?" I asked, now armed with a pen and paper.

"Well, she owned nearly twenty percent of an app that was developed by a think tank here in Michigan," Nate said. "It had something to do with phone messaging, I'm not sure. Anyway, Microsoft bought it for nearly a billion dollars."

Math isn't exactly my strong suit, but I let out a low whistle and said, "So she made close to a couple hundred million on the deal?"

"Yep."

"Huh."

"But she'd had some hits and misses until she started doing well again, and more consistently," he continued. "She had a string of ventures that nearly all paid out quite handsomely."

There was a wonderful edge in his voice and I knew it was the reason he called.

"They all had to do with a single industry."

I knew what he was going to say before he said it.

"Medical."

CHAPTER EIGHTEEN

The Point beer tasted so good I decided to double-check my judgment by having another.

Nate's information rattled around in my brain. Colleen Fairbanks was a venture capitalist recently specializing in medical investments.

Nick Giordano was a highly-regarded neurologist with a successful practice who'd been spending less time in the office.

It suddenly occurred to me to wonder if Nick had been a medical convention kind of guy. Weren't doctors famous for jetting off to places like Vegas and the southern coast of France?

Hell, I wouldn't have blamed him. I'd only been to one law enforcement convention in my life, in Chicago and it had been a lot of fun. Way too much fun–

I slammed the beer down on my desk and sat straight up in my chair.

Holy shit.

The blonde woman with spiked hair. The one who'd been

following me in the black Impala on my trip out to see Dr. Rieghels.

I knew who she was.

It was difficult for me to believe, but it had to be true.

She was a private investigator.

Which meant that someone had hired her to keep tabs on me.

I'm not going to lie, it chapped my ass big time. I didn't appreciate it at all. I was a guy just trying to do his job and do it well. What motivation could anyone have to keep track of where I was going and what I was doing?

Again, a pang of guilt came with the answer.

Katie Giordano.

She had been openly rude to me during my questioning. She clearly hadn't been eager to help. And she had the means, i.e., plenty of money, to hire someone.

Plus, it was pretty clear that she just didn't like me and the idea that I was digging around in her husband's murder case probably pissed her off even more.

Or maybe my instant reaction was because I was fresh from my conversation with Frederick about the trip to Napa. Had he called her? Or was I just being paranoid?

Maybe it wasn't Katie at all. Maybe it was a former client of mine. Or maybe a criminal I had helped build a case against.

But something told me I wasn't being paranoid. That I was, in fact, correct.

Well, goddamn it now I was riled up. It was time to talk to Katie again. And this time, I wouldn't be so nice.

CHAPTER NINETEEN

I parked outside the Giordano house, rang the doorbell and waited. No one came to the door. I didn't see any signs of life inside, just stacks of boxes from L.L. Bean, Nordstrom and Gucci.

Back behind the wheel of my car, I drove around the block, and then pulled up on the opposite side and parked along the curb. From what I heard, Katie enjoyed going shopping at malls when she needed a break from online shopping.

The best mall in Detroit was Somerset Mall in Troy, but even if she was there, I was willing to wait for her to return. She and I had a few things to talk about.

I sat there for two hours, playing a game on my phone called Trivia Crack and occasionally checking email. I seemed to attract email from people with large sums of inheritance money or people looking for a fuck buddy. Whatever that was.

At the end of the two-hour mark Katie pulled into the driveway in her giant Lexus SUV. They had an underground garage so I waited until she parked inside, the door closed and then I paused again so she would have plenty of time to bring up all the packages and pile them on top of all the other packages in the house.

Finally, I got out of my car, crossed the street and rang the front doorbell again.

Katie opened the door and rolled her eyes.

"I don't really have time for this," she said. She had a huge red wine glass nearly full. That thing had to hold at least half of a bottle of wine.

"It won't take more than a minute or two," I said. "Just a couple of quick questions."

She stepped back just far enough to let me inside but not far enough to indicate that I was welcome any farther than just a foot or two inside the door.

"Did you hire this person to follow me?" I asked. I had grabbed the woman's photo from her website. Her name was Sky Farrow, which sounded as genuine as Katie's horrible hair extensions that I had suddenly noticed and couldn't stop looking at. They were a completely different color than the hair on top of her head. I was just a guy, but it seemed to me that was a mistake.

Katie glanced at my phone and then shrugged her shoulders indifferently. "Nope," she said.

I took that as a big yes.

"Why?" I asked.

"You said you had two questions," she replied. "Is 'why' the second and final one?"

She clearly had no intention of answering either one. So I went for a third.

"What was the name of the group you were with in Napa? It was a wine-tasting tour, right?"

She stepped past me, opened the door.

"You were always a disgrace to the family," she said. "Nick always talked about how embarrassed he was that his sister married such a loser like you," she said. Her voice was getting louder and higher-pitched. It sounded like mental instability. "You killed someone, for Christ's sake. An innocent boy you were supposed to protect. I'm done with you. Forever."

She slammed the door shut and I had to jump back to avoid having my nose broken.

I looked on the bright side.

The next Giordano family reunion was going to be a hoot!

CHAPTER TWENTY

Probably because of the guilt I'd felt about prying some information out of Frederick I decided against calling either him or Paul to try to get more information on their mother's trip to Napa. Besides, Frederick hadn't been very eager to discuss it, anyway.

So I went back to my office, decided against cracking open another Point and Googled the hell out of Katie Giordano.

The results were nearly nonexistent.

The only real hits on her name were a couple of mentions of the annual fundraiser at their kids' elite, private school in Grosse Pointe. For several years running, the most expensive prize at the auction was bid on and won by, you guessed it, Katie Giordano. One year it was a trip to Europe. Another time it was a cruise to Hawaii.

Of course, knowing what I did about Katie, the real prize at those school auctions had been the joy of rubbing all of her husband's money in everyone's face. Hell, I wondered if Nick had even gone on any of those trips. It didn't seem to me like he'd been all that eager to spend any time with her.

Gee, I couldn't understand why.

With little hope, I closed the Google window and tried Facebook.

Nothing.

The next step was to try her maiden name. It took me awhile to remember it, but then it came to me. Wolter. Katie Wolter. If I remembered correctly, she had originally been from Toronto and had gone to school in the U.S. where she'd met Nick.

So I typed in Katie Wolter.

Once again, the Internet drew a blank.

And then I wondered if Katie was short for anything. Of course it was. I'm sure there were people who named their daughter Katie, and Katie only. But I was guessing that for most, it was short for something.

My first guess hit the jackpot: Katherine Wolter.

Many pages of Google hits.

And a personal Facebook page.

The Facebook page was intriguing, but her privacy settings only allowed me to see a few things. For instance, I could see one of the names of the folders holding photographs, but I couldn't see the pictures themselves.

One of the folders was called Napa.

Damn, I needed to see those photos.

Something I had noticed with Katie, in addition to her giant wine glass, she frequently had her phone in hand and at one point when she was kicking me out of her house I was fairly certain I saw the Facebook layout on her phone. Facebook mobile.

It wouldn't have surprised me if she was one of those middle-aged people who were always wasting time on Facebook, posting every single highlight of their lives and never mentioning the shitstorm that at some point everyone on

Earth endured. Instead, they focused on how many "Likes" their posts received.

As if any of that mattered.

Some time ago, I had bought a group of one hundred emails from the service provider that hosted my website. Using those emails, I had, on one weekend at the office, set up nearly a dozen fake Facebook accounts with them.

With a goal in mind, I had tried to figure out every age, gender, and interest group I might need for future cases. Sometimes they could come in handy for someone who didn't want to talk to me, but had no problem sharing stuff on social media.

Which was a very common affliction these days.

Now, I looked at my aliases and wondered what the best one would be to use. Maybe it was the cynic in me, but it sounded like Nick and Katie hadn't had the best marriage and even though she had been recently widowed in the worst possible way, I thought there might be a chance that she was open to meeting new men. Especially new, ruggedly handsome men.

'Ted Stanchion' was one of my favorite Facebook accounts. I'd used a royalty free stock image for his profile picture. It was a candid photo of a man in his late forties, possibly early fifties with salt and pepper hair, a finely chiseled jaw and a five o'clock shadow.

He was wearing a white shirt, rolled up jeans and he was on the deck of a sailboat. He looked like he was about to sail up to the Kennedy compound and be welcomed inside as a dear friend of the family.

I'd had some fun with 'Ted Stanchion.' The guy had a sense of humor but he was kind of dumb, clumsy and a bit arrogant.

Needless to say, lonely middle-aged women (and some men) loved Ted Stanchion.

Ted sent Katie a friend request and I grabbed another Point beer, set my feet up on the desk and waited.

Twenty minutes later, unbeknownst to her, Katie and I were friends again.

CHAPTER TWENTY-ONE

The first thing that became apparent to me as Katherine Wolter's new Facebook friend? She didn't have a lot of friends.

It looked like most of them were from Toronto and I guessed that meant family or friends of family. She had very few Grosse Pointe friends.

Shocker.

But when I clicked on her "Likes" that's where I saw all of her passions. Every store conceivable was listed as a favorite of Katie's. From fashion to cooking to travel and jewelry. It was like she automatically liked the top five hundred retailers in the world.

Which probably wasn't much of a stretch.

But what I wanted to see were the pictures in the Napa folder. There were only three, which I found incredibly disappointing. One of them was of Katie by herself, standing in front of a building but only the edge of the structure was visible.

The second picture was of Katie a large, manly-looking

woman who had her arm around her. This was taken on a hill overlooking a valley.

The third picture was of Katie with a man who looked vaguely similar to the manly woman. They were standing on a hill and in the background I could just barely make out a gate with a sign at the top. I had to do a screen grab of the image and then use a photo tool to magnify the image and sharpen the focus.

I could just barely make out the words.

Napa Restorative Services.

CHAPTER TWENTY-TWO

Not much online could be found about Napa Restorative Services. I couldn't find the name of any employees or even a website. All I had was the photo and the belief that it was somewhere in northern California.

In a database of California businesses, I was eventually able to find an address and when I Google mapped it, the surrounding terrain matched what I'd seen in Katie's photograph.

There was no phone number and no email address, which I found very odd for a business.

How did they get new customers? How had Katie found them? And why didn't they have normal ways to get in touch? Was it just a matter of being exclusive? Or was there some other kind of answer?

In my opinion, there was only one way to find out.

CHAPTER TWENTY-THREE

"This is some kind of joke, right?" Anna said.

News of my decision to take a trip to Napa wasn't going over all that well at home.

I explained what I'd learned so far, and even though I had carefully explained the situation, it seemed my wife didn't entirely believe that I needed to go to one of the most beautiful places in the country on business.

"No, no joke," I said. "I'll only be gone a day or two and I promise to bring back as much wine as they'll let me bring on the plane. And I'll try not to drink it on the way home."

The flights were cheap mainly because I used a bargain travel service that had unsold tickets and I found a cheap hotel by the airport.

All it took was one suitcase that would fit in the overhead compartment and some extra cash. With a quick goodbye to the girls and a peck on Anna's cheek, I headed out to the car. The airport was only a half hour away and I had more than enough time to get there, but I was a nervous traveler. Always had been, always would be. I pulled up to Mack Avenue on Cadieux, the border between Grosse Pointe and Detroit, just as a squad car's lights went on behind me. I pulled over to let him by, but he followed me over to the curb.

What the hell?

Then I smiled. It had to be Ellen. She'd done this before, plus, I'd barely been going the friggin' speed limit. I never sped in Grosse Pointe, they loved to give speeding tickets left and right. Kept the police department well funded.

I checked my rearview mirror, expecting to see Ellen sauntering up to my car and I wasn't disappointed. She approached with a hand on the butt of her pistol. Suddenly, I was a tiny bit worried. I rolled down the window and gave her my license and registration which she didn't take.

"Put that away, dumb ass," she said.

"Was I speeding?" I asked.

"One more question and I'll shoot you," she answered.

Again, what the hell?

I decided keeping quiet might be the best option here.

Ellen opened the rear door and reached into the back seat. She pulled out a baggie.

At first, I figured it was from one of the girls' lunches. You know, a little piece of crust from one of their peanut butter and jelly sandwiches. Their lunch bags sometimes ended up all over the place.

But when Ellen held up the baggie, I could see there wasn't a sandwich inside.

The little plastic bag was tied at the top and I could see a small lump of brownish white powder.

As I watched, she pulled out a little kit, put a touch of the powder in and shook it up. It turned blue, which matched the exact color of my face, probably.

Ellen turned to me.

"Follow me, Meth Boy."

CHAPTER TWENTY-FOUR

"I guess the good thing about you being on meth is you might actually get something done," Ellen pointed out. "You know, more energy. Maybe you'll actually get some work done around the house, I'll let Anna know."

Ellen smiled at me, her face beaming with positivity. We were sitting in her office. "You might even lose some weight, too, which I think would be great for you. I've noticed just a little bit of a love handle going on there—"

"Ellen, can we be serious for a minute?" I asked, not really believing those words had just come out of my mouth.

"You meth heads have no sense of humor," she answered.

"It was obviously planted," I said. "I think I even know by who."

"Do tell."

"Sky Farrow. A scumbag private investigator famous for dirty tricks. I think she was hired by Katie Giordano to get me off the case."

Ellen leaned back in her chair.

"The call was anonymous," Ellen said. "But when the dispatcher told me about it, I thought I would come and find out. Rather than spending good taxpayer money on something that was obviously a hoax."

"What'd the caller say?"

"That a guy named John Rockne was heading to the airport with a stash of drugs in his backseat." Ellen shook her head. "It was the best joke I'd ever heard. My brother John an international drug dealer. Hell, Anna doesn't trust you to pick up the kids' prescriptions at CVS."

I was glad my sister was enjoying this, but I had a few very grave concerns.

For starters: *How did they know I was going to the airport?*

"She bugged my office," I said.

"Who?"

"Sky Farrow."

The bitch.

Now I was mad.

"Well, if they call back I'll just say that their tip didn't pan out, then try to get more information."

"Was it actually meth?" I asked.

"I'm afraid so, John," she sighed. "Enough that you would've gotten at least ten years. If your sister wasn't such a frickin' angel."

These pricks were playing for keeps.

"Am I free to go?"

"Sure," Ellen said. "As long as you promise me one thing."

"What's that?"

"Get your head out of your ass."

CHAPTER TWENTY-FIVE

Needless to say, the flight was missed.

I headed home, went to bed late and got up early. Anna joined me for coffee after a bit. I told her what happened.

"Jesus John, someone isn't messing around," she said. Her face became angry. "First they kill my brother, now they try to frame my husband so he might go to prison for a dozen years or so?"

Her hand gripped the coffee mug so hard I thought it might shatter in her hands. I reached over, pulled her hand away and held it in my own.

"This is a good sign," I said. "When they're getting scared, that means we're getting close."

In fact, I was now more determined than ever to fly out to California and find out exactly what the hell this Napa Restorative Services was all about.

Since it seemed like a priority of theirs, whoever they might be, to keep me from getting to the airport. I went up to my computer, launched my web browser and started looking for another flight.

But before I got that far, the local news page popped onto

my screen and I had to blink several times to understand what I was looking at.

Oscar Shaw, head of Napa Restorative Services, was doing a program at the Grosse Pointe War Memorial on the health benefits of California. It seemed Napa Restorative Services was billing itself as a cross between a spa and a winery, adding a quasi-mental health aspect to the enterprise.

I immediately closed my browser.

It occurred to me that this group must have come to Grosse Pointe before and that's how Katie most likely found them.

It never ceased to amaze me how much stuff could be going on in such a small town like Grosse Pointe that I never knew about.

Well, at least they had saved me the trouble of an expensive flight.

CHAPTER TWENTY-SIX

The Grosse Pointe War Memorial is located right off of Jefferson Avenue. It used to be a home owned by one of the early wealthy Grosse Pointe families that had eventually been donated to the city.

It was located on the banks of Lake St. Clair and afforded gorgeous views from multiple rooms sporting giant windows designed just for that purpose.

I parked in the expansive parking lot and once again marveled at the beauty of the building. To imagine it had once been a private home was impressive.

Once inside, I followed the signs to the Napa Restorative Services wine hour. It was being held in a room just off the main hallway that featured a parquet floor and floor-to-ceiling bookshelves. Several large oil paintings adorned the walls and at the opposite end of the room a massive fireplace.

There was a wooden podium at the front of the room and about two dozen chairs set out facing the front.

I saw a lot of heads with white hair, and the audience was overwhelmingly female. I saw Katie Giordano sitting at the front of the room.

I took a seat in back.

A server wearing a white shirt and black slacks brought a tray with glasses of wine around and I selected one.

There was no one I knew in the audience, and Katie never looked back at me. I figured when she saw me she might have a problem with my presence.

Eventually, a man I guessed to be in his late fifties with obviously colored hair walked to the front of the podium.

"Cheers everyone!" he sang out and took a drink of wine.

"My name is Oscar Shaw and I am the founder of Napa Restorative Services. Let me start off by telling you what my talk will NOT be," he smiled. And he had a set of dazzling white chompers. I could practically hear some of the older ladies twitter at the sight of his smile. I took a closer look at Oscar Shaw and noticed the tight-fitting slacks and shirt, the ropy musculature of his arms and the expensive watch on his left wrist.

The guy was a player, through and through. If money were even, I'd bet that these older rich ladies from Grosse Pointe were easy pickings for him. And even some of the slightly younger ones, i.e. Katie.

"The session will not be lengthy," he said and some of the ladies chuckled. "It will not be a sales pitch, because I am not a salesman. I am a wine lover," he said.

"I will not even be specific about what we do at NRS, suffice to say, we don't have a website, nor do we publicly advertise. In fact, the program is invitation only," he announced. His voice was as smooth as honey. "Even if you wanted to, you couldn't join."

I almost laughed. It was the reverse selling technique.

This made me ready for the sales pitch that had to be coming.

"Let me just show you a short video of my place in California," he said.

Ah, the non-sales sales pitch.

What followed was a five-minute video showing breath-taking shots of Napa Valley, an infinity pool, beautiful-looking people getting spa treatments, musical entertainment, gourmet meals and meditation circles, along with yoga and tai chi. All set under a warm sun and blue skies. I half expected to see ghost-like angels flitting in the air above the people.

But like all good salesmen, Oscar Shaw saved the best for last.

I could tell this guy knew how to close a sales pitch.

Because the real selling points were some celebrity testi-monials. These mostly B-listers provided short statements documenting how time spent with Oscar Shaw and NRS changed their lives, focused them on their business careers, and revved up their sex lives.

The last part surprised me.

I felt a little tingle at the back of my neck. The cynic in me wondered, is this guy recruiting rich old Grosse Pointe ladies to go out to Napa, drink wine and have orgies?

The servers came around again with more wine, some cheese, and some cards.

I took a card and reviewed it.

It was a request for all kinds of information, including something that seemed a bit personal, like estimated net worth.

"What's being brought around now is essentially a card you can fill out, or not, if you don't want to, and some of my favorite wine," Oscar Shaw intoned. "A nutty chardonnay from my own personal label. It is accompanied by some cheese I get from an organic farm near the winery, and a card with some information you can provide if you wish."

He beamed out at his audience. I could tell he'd won the crowd over. People were smiling and laughing, the ladies' faces were flushed.

"We will review the information and please take your time filling it out," Shaw said. "There is a blank space in which you can write why you are interested in NRS, and that is one of the biggest things we look at when determining if you might be a good fit for us and vice versa."

I almost laughed.

I had a feeling the net worth item was the only thing this scumbag looked at.

I saw the majority of women filling out the information. The only other men there, two older guys, were just downing glasses of wine, encouraging their wives to fill out the cards, probably hoping they'd head out west so they could have a couple weeks golfing. Whatever it took in old age, I guess.

At the end, we watched another short video and I felt a little odd from the last glass of wine. The one that had come from his personal estate.

I actually felt myself get a little sexually aroused, especially when the video was playing. Now, some of the people in the video were really quite striking, and there was one pool scene where there seemed to be an abundance of exposed flesh. I wondered why I felt the sudden physical reaction. Was it the video? Or was there something in the wine? An aphrodisiac? Or was it a carefully orchestrated combination of the two?

Once the presentation was over and the ladies in the audience descended on Oscar Shaw, I decided to avoid confronting the guy and Katie, and instead, went out to the car and waited. I had a very good inclination of where they would be going at the end of the program.

My head was pleasantly buzzing from the wine, and I have to admit it felt pretty damn good, even though I was a beer guy through and through.

My hunch paid off because sure enough I saw Oscar Shaw and Katie emerge from the building, get into her Lexus and I followed them back to Katie's house. Using my phone I snapped some photos of the two getting out of the car and going into the house.

Not only did I now have some fairly good photographic evidence, I had something even more important.

I had a motive.

I was about to put my car into gear when a shadow fell across my window. The door was yanked open and a guy with the face of a slab of granite pulled me out.

Luckily, I had slipped my phone into the compartment below the radio.

"Are you loitering?" he said.

"No, I was about to leave until you did this," I answered.

"Okay," he said and let me go. His hands were like giant meat hooks.

"I don't want to see you around here again," he said.

It would have been a good time to ask him exactly what he meant. Around here? Like, all of Grosse Pointe?

Instead, I got into the car and shut the door.

For a brief moment, I considered backing up and running the giant over, but I figured my car might end up being the loser in that confrontation.

CHAPTER TWENTY-SEVEN

I called Ellen and said I wanted her to swing by my office for a beer before the end of the day.

After a quick check of my watch, I realized it was time to meet with Nate and pay him for his research services.

He had asked to change the location from Green Dot Stables in Detroit to the Thai place in the village since he was on his way home.

There was a booth available so I took it, along with two menus. I was determined to have the tofu salad. I read that tofu was supposed to take cholesterol out of the blood stream. Not that I had a problem with cholesterol, but mostly because I wanted to show Nate how someone with restraint eats.

He had always been a big guy, but lately the pounds were adding up and I was worried about him. He had a beautiful wife and daughter and although he was a grown man capable of making his own choices, I wanted to help however I could. The direct approach hadn't worked in the past. It just pissed him off and now I was forbidden by him to say anything

about his weight, even though we were each other's best
friend.

Right on time, he walked into the restaurant and joined
me in the booth.

We ordered our food and then the first thing he said took
me by surprise.

"Brian Fairbanks," he said. "Do you know anything
about him?"

I told him what I'd learned. That he was a rich guy,
involved in auto stuff, and eventually developed a lot of envi-
ronmentally friendly car things and started his own company.
His car was one of the leading candidates to revolutionize the
electric car industry.

Some of the big, national magazines had done profiles on
the guy.

"Yeah, that's all accurate," Nate said. "But before all of
that, Brian had some problems," he said, spearing some fried
rolls our server had just placed on the table.

Screw my tofu, I thought, and took a couple of the rolls.
Damn they were good.

"He had a reputation for fighting, a lot," Nate continued.
"And then he got into some drug issues in college, dropped
out, and disappeared for awhile."

"Disappeared where?" I asked.

"Eventually, he surfaced in Europe, working for Fiat," he
said around a mouthful of spring roll. "That's where he had
his turnaround and then he came back. When he met
Colleen, he had a lot of ideas. She helped fund his shit, and
then all of that really took off."

I noodled that around, along with some spicy noodles. I
asked the waitress to take away the tofu monstrosity. If I
wanted something like it, I could go home and eat some card-
board from our home office.

"But he's been clean ever since?" I asked.

Nate nodded.

"So do you buy he's a changed man?" I wondered.

"I do, but if I were you, I would find out for myself," Nate said. "He does most of his work at a building near Chrysler headquarters. Couldn't be too hard to arrange a meeting."

After we finished, I called and did just that, explaining who I was, and requiring a couple of callbacks to verify my identity. It was to be tomorrow morning.

Nate and I finished our meal and talked about family stuff, setting the details of the two crimes aside. It was always good to see him.

We said our goodbyes and then I went back to my office, organized all of my thoughts on the case and ran through a lot of scenarios.

By the time I was done, there was a knock on the door and Ellen walked in.

"Beer me," she said.

CHAPTER TWENTY-EIGHT

"Oscar Shaw," I said, and then proceeded to tell Ellen what I'd discovered about Katie, the guy from Napa, and although it was a good story, my sister summarily dismissed most of it.

"Doesn't sound like the kind of guy that would set up two long-range sniper shots," she said. "Besides, it would be fairly easy to check out where he was at the time of both murders, if he's traveling back and forth from Napa. Something tells me he's going to have an airtight alibi." She took a sip of her beer and looked at the picture I'd grabbed from the Internet of Shaw.

She laughed. "What did he do, use a crate of wine as his tripod to rest the rifle?"

She had a point.

Oscar Shaw didn't really fit the scenario as the actual shooter, but that didn't necessarily mean he wasn't involved somehow.

When it was her turn, she told me what they'd found. The .223 bullets were in fact impossible to trace. She'd gone over the crime scene photos from the Colleen Fairbanks killing and it was almost exactly the same as Nick's. No evidence. No one had seen anything. No hard evidence. Just a ballistics match.

They'd already known about Colleen Fairbanks's husband, as well as his criminal background.

"I think you're wasting your time on that one," she said. "He wasn't even in the country when his wife was killed. The financial guys who worked the case went over all of his money, looking for a murder-for-hire scenario and came up with nothing."

She did have one surprise for me though.

"We were given some footage from Colleen Fairbanks's office from the day before she was killed," Ellen said. "It wasn't great quality but very interesting nonetheless."

"And?"

"It was Nick Giordano. At her office," Ellen said. "He spent at least a couple of hours, and then they left together. It was around lunchtime. But they didn't come back the rest of the day."

Finally, proof that Nick and Colleen Fairbanks had *some* kind of relationship.

It clicked right into place, I had to admit. It sure looked like Katie had found something to do with Oscar Shaw out in Napa, and it made sense that Nick might have been looking for some companionship as well. I had a question.

"So do you think it was business, personal, or both?" I already had my opinion, but I wanted to hear hers.

Ellen shrugged. "It could mean a lot either way. But the fact they never came back to the office that day suggests it was either a long meeting, or something much more than that."

The fact that she invested in medical-type things made sense it was business, but I hadn't been able to find evidence that suggested Nick was creating anything she was interested in.

Unless Colleen Fairbanks wasn't focused on something Nick was inventing.

Maybe she was just interested in Nick.

CHAPTER TWENTY-NINE

There was another conversation I had to have, even though I felt bad putting him through it all again. But there was no choice. I drove into downtown Detroit and knocked on the door of Frederick Giordano's condo. I checked my watch. 7 p.m. and the door opened.

I instantly caught a whiff of marijuana smoke. And his eyes looked a little red.

"Uncle John," he said with a mixture of surprise and what my intuition determined might be guilt. Frederick stepped aside to let me in.

I walked into the condo and saw Paul Giordano lounged in a chair.

He got up and shook my hand.

"This is great," I said. "I really wanted to talk to both of you."

There was a girl standing in the kitchen area, a dark-haired beauty who excused herself and went into another room.

I sat down and Frederick offered me a beer, which I took.

Whoever had been smoking pot had hidden the evidence.

"I thought you were in Chicago," I said to Paul.

"Yeah, I came back," he said. "Just to check out an invest-ment we might make in a building here in town. And to keep an eye on Frederick, you know. He's trouble." Paul smiled his easy smile and I was reminded again of how much he looked like his father. Paul had such an easy charm about him.

Frederick nodded. "I've gotten really good at picking out distressed properties, and there's an old factory here that used to make wheels for Ford. Perfect property to convert to lofts."

There was no good way to ask it so I just got down to business.

"Do you know if your Dad's relationship with Colleen Fairbanks was anything more than just business?"

Frederick looked at Paul, who looked away from the tele-vision set and out the window.

Frederick stood up, went into the kitchen and poured himself a glass of wine.

Paul looked back at me, then at Frederick.

Finally, he sighed.

"Yeah," Paul said. "We think he was in love with her."

CHAPTER THIRTY

"We don't have proof," Paul continued. "But Frederick and I both agree that he was a different guy during the past year or so."

"Different how?"

Frederick shrugged his shoulders and looked at Paul.

"Dad didn't really talk to us about any of that kind of stuff. He always talked about us, pushed us to be successful. His private life was private. But he acted like he was in love. We both agree to that."

Paul looked at Frederick and Frederick nodded in agreement.

We talked for a little longer but I could get nothing more from either one of them. I believed they were telling me the truth.

With the suggestion to call me if they thought of anything else, I left and decided to throw caution to the wind and drive out to talk with Brian Fairbanks directly. Nate's research provided me the address and when I pulled up to the expansive home in the sprawling Bloomfield Hills neighborhood, I wasn't surprised. It looked exactly like the kind of place a

successful venture capitalist would live with her auto execu-
tive husband.

Brian Fairbanks answered the door wearing slacks, a sport
coat, and holding a glass of scotch.

"Mr. Fairbanks? I'm John Rockne, a private investigator
looking into the murder of Nick Giordano."

He looked at me, almost a bemused smile on his face. He
was a big guy, with a ruddy complexion and a fairly good-sized
spare tire hanging over his belt.

"I'll give you two minutes," he said.

He leaned against the doorframe and waited for me to ask
my questions.

"Okay," I said.

"This is going to be a really short conversation," he said
before I could even get out the first question. "I'm going to
answer most of your questions with one word. So ask wisely.
This interview will be over as soon as I decide it's over."

He had a deep, baritone voice and he spoke with the kind
of casual authority that told me he was very used to being the
boss and in complete control.

"Was your wife having an affair?" Hey, if I was going to be
limited in my questions, I figured I should start with a doozy.

"Yes."

"With who?"

"Unknown."

He took a drink of his scotch and for a second I thought
he was going to slam the door shut, so I hurried along with
my next question.

"Was she having more than one affair?" I asked.

"Yes."

"Were you going to divorce?"

"Yes."

"Was one of the men she was seeing Nick Giordano?"

He actually thought for a moment.

"No."

"Did you kill her?"

"No."

"Did you have her killed?"

"No."

Now it was my turn to hesitate. These one-word answers weren't going to help me in the long run. So I tried to ask a question that required more.

"Who do you think killed her?"

"Unknown."

So much for that strategy.

He drained the rest of his scotch.

"Interview is over."

He turned and grabbed the edge of the door.

I held up my hand.

"You only hesitated on one question," I said. "I asked you if one of the men was Nick Giordano. You said no, but you hesitated first. Why?"

He looked through the doorway toward the street out front. Just when I thought he was never going to answer he turned to me with a tired smile.

"He was way too old for her."

CHAPTER THIRTY-ONE

One of the nice things about Nick Giordano's house was that by being so near the lake, it made taking long walks in the evening along the water so easy.

After ringing the doorbell and waiting, looking into the garage and seeing the Lexus, I decided that maybe Katie and Oscar Shaw had decided to go for a walk.

It was early evening now and the sky above the lake had just the slightest tinge of orange at the far horizon. Across the water, I could see the edge of Canada and the windmills they had installed a few years back.

I walked to the edge of the lake and looked to my left. There was a path that ran along the bank haphazardly before petering out at the property line of the nearest house.

To my right, the sidewalk meandered back into the neighborhoods before reappearing at the edge of the park.

There were two people walking together, not holding hands, but close enough to suggest an intimacy. I set off after them and when I got closer I could see that the couple was, in fact, Katie and Oscar Shaw.

"Hello," I said as I caught up to them.

They both turned and Katie's face went nearly white with rage. I saw her jaw harden and she stepped forward.

But then something bizarre happened.

Oscar Shaw put his hands on Katie's shoulders and she seemed to nearly melt at his touch. It was as if the anger completely left her body and the pale fury in her face was almost instantaneously replaced with warmth.

"What can we do for you?" Shaw said, with that honey-smooth voice he'd used for the old folks at the War Memorial.

"How much of your money are you giving this guy?" I asked Katie.

"Nothing," they said in unison.

Shaw seemed puzzled.

"Why do you ask that?" he said.

I've been lied to by so many people I've lost track so I have a good appreciation for good liars. Oscar Shaw was smooth.

"I'm not buying all that bullshit you're selling," I said. "Your whole pitch was ridiculous. But it worked on Katie, didn't it?"

"I'm not selling anything other than healing," Shaw said. "I've always been totally clear on that."

"What did you need to heal from?" I asked Katie.

She tensed again, but Shaw's hands seemed to soothe her and the rage that briefly flashed across her face was gone immediately.

"The end of my marriage. The end of my family," she answered.

I was surprised she answered at all considering what she said to me the last time we spoke.

Oscar Shaw looked at me.

"Katie had nothing to do with any of this," he said. "I understand you're an investigator and I can tell you, this path of investigation will not lead you to Nick Giordano's killer. Katie is only interested in rebuilding her relationship with her sons right now."

Damn it. I believed the guy.

Something wasn't adding up. If Shaw was exactly who he said he was—

And then a chill swept through my body that was so cold and powerful for a brief moment I thought it came from the lake.

Her sons.

But it hadn't.

I thought about what Brian Fairbanks had told me. How he had been so sure that Nick hadn't been having an affair with Colleen Fairbanks.

The ramifications ricocheted around my brain and I found myself backing away from Shaw and Katie. I turned and walked away as the different pieces finally fell into place.

It couldn't be.

But I had one way of finding out if I was right.

I turned and began running to my car, dialing Ellen's cell phone on the way.

CHAPTER THIRTY-TWO

I barged into the police station, headed for the media room. When I got there, Ellen was at the computer screen, staring at the image of Nick Giordano leaving with Colleen Fairbanks.

Stocker and Radcliffe looked at me.

"What's he doing here?" Stocker said.

"It was his idea," Ellen answered, without any emotion.

I stood behind them and looked at the screen.

"Is this the footage from Colleen Fairbanks's building? The one you said showed Nick was there?"

"It is," Ellen said.

"The detectives on that case sent it to us," she said. "They were confident it was Nick, but never able to prove it."

The footage was from two security cameras, one inside the building, and one outside.

It showed Nick walking into the camera's view from the parking lot, then into the building. The footage had then been edited to show Nick coming back out of the building with Colleen, and walking off-camera into the parking lot.

Ellen used the keyboard to toggle back and forth.

"Never got a good look at his face," Stocker said. "But it sure looks like Nick Giordano."

Everything I suspected jumped out from the screen.

"That's not Nick," I said.

I thought back to what Brian Fairbanks had told me.

"Colleen Fairbanks's husband told me that Nick Giordano was not having an affair with his wife."

"Yeah, so what? How would he have known?" Stocker asked, his voice full of skepticism.

"He said that Nick would have been way too old for Colleen."

Ellen, Stocker and Radcliffe turned, looked at the image, then back at me.

I nodded.

"That's not Nick Giordano. It's Paul Giordano. His son."

CHAPTER THIRTY-THREE

I rode with Ellen to Frederick's apartment, and after she and Stocker and Radcliffe entered, I was allowed to join them.

Frederick was sitting in the same chair Paul had been sitting in, but now his face was a bloodied mess, and there were liquor bottles on the floor and the smell of pot was even stronger.

"Where is Paul?" Ellen asked him.

"I don't know," Frederick said. He was completely dazed and I didn't know if it was from the liquor, the marijuana or the beating he had clearly taken.

"Who was the girl that was here before?" I asked.

Ellen looked at me, then back to Frederick.

"What girl?" she asked.

"Francine?" Frederick said to me.

He looked at me, and I waited patiently. "Her name is Francine," he said. "My girlfriend. She flew back to New York yesterday."

"Where's Paul?" Ellen asked.

Stocker and Radcliffe walked around the apartment, looking at anything that might tell them where Paul was.

I watched Frederick wrestle with the question.

"I don't know," he finally said.

"He's probably on his way back to Chicago," Stocker said. "That's where he lives, right?"

With a shake of my head I said, "No, I don't think so."

Stocker snorted. "Okay genius, then where is he?"

Everyone in the room looked at me. Chicago just didn't make sense. Everything he cared about was here. In fact, I had a pretty good idea of why he'd killed both Colleen Fairbanks and his father.

And it had nothing to do with Chicago.

"Come on, spit it out, Super Star," Stocker said.

Ellen started to say something to him, but I waved her off.

It had been Katie's comment about rebuilding her relationship with her sons that had helped me put it all together. There had been something about the way she said it, with Oscar Shaw standing behind her, and in the background, the lake—

Just as suddenly, I knew where Paul was.

CHAPTER THIRTY-FOUR

Nick's sailboat had been processed and then returned to the Grosse Pointe Park Marina.

The marina was less than a quarter mile from Nick's house, which had probably made it convenient for him to buy the boat and use it in the first place.

It had also made me wonder if that's why Katie and Oscar were walking toward the park, which housed the marina. When Shaw had mentioned Katie's sons, it struck a chord with me. Maybe their walk wasn't aimless. Maybe instead, she was walking somewhere to work on her relationship with Paul, *at that very moment*.

We pulled into the marina's parking lot, a group of Grosse Pointe police cars with lights flashing, but sirens on silent.

It was cooler now and the park was empty.

We got out of Ellen's car and jogged toward the marina. There were still a few boats in their slips, even though most had been taken out already.

Nick Giordano's sailboat was in the middle of the marina.

A quick glance told me the boat was big enough to have a

cabin that could serve as a place to hide out. I figured it also had a toilet, and maybe even a basic cooking area.

If Paul had wanted a place to think about what had happened, and maybe think about escaping, a boat wasn't a bad idea.

Two other Grosse Pointe policemen had taken positions at the entrance to the marina to make sure no one entered or left until Ellen got there.

Once again, I followed Ellen, Stocker and Radcliffe past the officers, and out onto the marina's slips.

We got to the boat, and Ellen tentatively stepped aboard, her service revolver out of its holster and in her hand.

Stocker and Radcliffe had also taken position with their guns, flanking Ellen.

I waited, closer to the entrance of the marina, near the two other officers.

I was close enough that I heard Ellen call out.

"Paul?" she said.

There was no answer.

I heard a voice from behind me and I looked back. Katie was running into the park, past the swimming pool toward the marina.

Oscar Shaw was trying to hold her back.

"No!" she yelled out.

I looked back at Ellen and she had moved closer to the sailboat's cabin.

"Paul, you have to turn yourself in, there's no other option."

But we all knew there was.

And Paul did, too.

Because just then, the boat rocked back and forth slightly and then a gunshot rang out.

Ellen ran forward, jumped into the space in front of the

sailboat's steering wheel and threw open the doors to the cabin. Stocker and Radcliffe followed her in.

We all waited.

Moments later, Ellen came back up.

She shook her head.

Katie screamed and fell to her knees, sobbing.

I knew then that Paul was dead.

CHAPTER THIRTY-FIVE

"It was Paul's idea, based on a suggestion by my Dad," Frederick explained to us.

We were sitting at my kitchen table. Anna, Ellen and Frederick.

Anna had made some pasta and now we were having an after-dinner drink.

"Dad had developed a portable device that could measure brain waves," Frederick explained. "He hadn't shared any of the details with me but I guess he had with Paul, because Paul went to school for engineering. And I guess it was something he had stumbled upon and wasn't exactly sure what it could mean."

Even before he told me the rest, I knew what was coming. It was money. Murder was almost always about money.

"Anyway, after he talked to Paul about it, Dad said he met Colleen Fairbanks somewhere and told her about the idea. She immediately saw how the device's application could be more than just a purely medical device, but one for everyday use."

"Kind of like those wristband exercise things?" I said.

"You could use one of those," Ellen said to me.

Anna laughed. She thought my sister was a hoot.

I didn't exactly share that sentiment.

"Exactly," Frederick told me. "So then Dad went back to Paul to tell him the good news, but Paul was furious. He didn't think they needed Colleen Fairbanks. In the process, he seduced her and tried to get her to back out of the deal."

Frederick shook his head. "But when she wouldn't do what he wanted, he killed her."

"Did your Dad put two and two together?" Ellen asked.

Frederick shook his head. "Hell no. Like I've said before, he hardly knew us. Which made him figure that there was no way Paul had anything to do with the woman's murder. But I knew Paul had always liked guns. It was like a secret hobby with him. If my Dad had ever been around, he would have known that, too."

"So why did he kill your Dad then?" I asked, even though I knew the answer.

"It was partly greed. And partly hate. He hated my Dad for never being around. I mean, our friends always assumed our parents were divorced because our Dad was never at anything. Parent-teacher conferences. Sporting events. Homecoming and prom. Nothing. Never around."

Frederick started crying.

"I swear I didn't know," he said. "He just told me and when I tried to get him to turn himself in, he went crazy, kicked my ass and left."

Anna put her arms around him.

"There was nothing you could have done," Anna said. "There was nothing any of us could have done."

CHAPTER THIRTY-SIX

I was parked outside the tiny office of Sky Investigations. It was an ugly brick building with a flat roof and bars on the windows and doors.

Down the alley there was a Chinese restaurant and a laundromat.

A bus stop was just up the street with several people milling around smoking cigarettes.

I had a nice cup of coffee in my hand and a smile on my face.

During questioning after Paul's suicide, Katie admitted she had hired Sky Farrow to keep tabs on me, but both she and Oscar Shaw swore they hadn't asked the woman to frame me.

Even better, they had recorded the meeting and after listening to the audio, I believed them.

What made things even better was the fact that my building had a security system and I was able to get footage of a woman dressed as an HVAC installer entering the front door of my office.

Combined with the listening devices detectives had found

on my office line and beneath my desk, there was more than enough to bring Sky Farrow in for questioning.

There probably wasn't enough to get a conviction, and even if she was found guilty, a good attorney would probably keep her from going to jail.

But still, a point needed to be made.

On cue, an unmarked squad car pulled up to the building. Two detectives got out of the car and knocked on the door.

Sky Farrow opened the door and after a brief conversation she was quickly placed in handcuffs.

I jumped out of my vehicle and ran to the unmarked car before they put her inside.

"Nice try," I said. "This isn't over, just so you know."

Her face was grim as they stashed her in the back seat of the unmarked car.

I raised my coffee cup to her and she mouthed something at me. It looked like she said a couple of words that were very naughty.

With an elaborate wink, I turned my back on her, got into my car and drove away.

Sky would definitely have some time to think about what she'd done.

Proof once again, that you should never mess with John Rockne.

THE END

ALSO BY DAN AMES

DEAD WOOD (John Rockne Mystery #1)

HARD ROCK (John Rockne Mystery #2)

COLD JADE (John Rockne Mystery #3)

LONG SHOT (John Rockne Mystery #4)

EASY PREY (John Rockne Mystery #5)

BODY BLOW (John Rockne Mystery #6)

THE KILLING LEAGUE (Wallace Mack Thriller #1)

THE MURDER STORE (Wallace Mack Thriller #2)

FINDERS KILLERS (Wallace Mack Thriller #3)

DEATH BY SARCASM (Mary Cooper Mystery #1)

MURDER WITH SARCASTIC INTENT (Mary Cooper
Mystery #2)

GROSS SARCASTIC HOMICIDE (Mary Cooper Mystery #3)

KILLER GROOVE (Rockne & Cooper Mystery #1)

BEER MONEY (Burr Ashland Mystery #1)

THE CIRCUIT RIDER (Circuit Rider #1)

KILLER'S DRAW (Circuit Rider #2)

TO FIND A MOUNTAIN (A WWII Thriller)

STANDALONE THRILLERS:

THE RECRUITER

KILLING THE RAT

HEAD SHOT

THE BUTCHER

BOX SETS:

AMES TO KILL

GROSSE POINTE PULP

GROSSE POINTE PULP 2

TOTAL SARCASM

WALLACE MACK THRILLER COLLECTION

SHORT STORIES:

THE GARBAGE COLLECTOR

BULLET RIVER

SCHOOL GIRL

HANGING CURVE

SCALE OF JUSTICE

AFTERWORD

THE JACK REACHER CASES

The JACK REACHER CASES
(A Hard Man To Forget)

A USA TODAY BESTSELLING BOOK

ABOUT THE AUTHOR

Dan Ames is a USA TODAY bestselling author and winner of the Independent Book Award for Crime Fiction.

www.authordanames.com
dan@authordanames.com

Made in the USA
Lexington, KY
10 April 2019